WHEELS ON THE BUS

Retold by STEVEN ANDERSON

Illustrated by GAIA BORDICCHIA

MANKATO, MINNESOTA

WWW.CANTATALEARNING.COM

CANTATA LEARNING
MANKATO, MINNESOTA

Published by Cantata Learning
1710 Roe Crest Drive
North Mankato, MN 56003
www.cantatalearning.com

Copyright © 2016 Cantata Learning

Library of Congress Control Number: 2014957032
978-1-63290-284-9 (hardcover/CD)
978-1-63290-436-2 (paperback/CD)
978-1-63290-478-2 (paperback)

Wheels on the Bus by Steven Anderson
Illustrated by Gaia Bordicchia

Book design, Tim Palin Creative
Editorial direction, Flat Sole Studio
Executive musical production and direction, Elizabeth Draper
Music arranged and produced by Steven C Music

Printed in the United States of America.

VISIT
WWW.CANTATALEARNING.COM/ACCESS-OUR-MUSIC
TO SING ALONG TO THE SONG

48
DOWNTOWN

4

How do people get around town?

Find out one way as you sing along!

Now turn the page, and sing along.

The wheels on the bus go

round and round,

round and round,

round and round.

The wheels on the bus go

round and round,

all through the town!

The people on the bus go

up and down,

up and down,

up and down.

The people on the bus go

up and down,

all through the town!

The horn on the bus goes

beep, beep, beep,

beep, beep, beep,

beep, beep, beep.

The horn on the bus goes

beep, beep, beep,

all through the town!

The **wipers** on the bus go

swish, swish, swish,

swish, swish, swish,

swish, swish, swish.

The wipers on the bus go

swish, swish, swish,

all through the town!

The **motor** on the bus goes

zoom, zoom, zoom,

zoom, zoom, zoom,

zoom, zoom, zoom.

The motor on the bus goes

zoom, zoom, zoom,

all through the town!

The babies on the bus go

waa, waa, waa,

waa, waa, waa,

waa, waa, waa.

The babies on the bus go

waa, waa, waa,

all through the town!

The parents on the bus go

shush, shush, shush,

shush, shush, shush,

shush, shush, shush.

The parents on the bus go

shush, shush, shush,

all through the town!

The wheels on the bus go

round and round,

round and round,

round and round.

The wheels on the bus go

round and round,

all through the town!

SONG LYRICS
Wheels on the Bus

The wheels on the bus go
round and round,
round and round,
round and round.

The wheels on the bus go
round and round,
all through the town!

The people on the bus go
up and down,
up and down,
up and down.

The people on the bus go
up and down,
all through the town!

The horn on the bus goes
beep, beep, beep,
beep, beep, beep,
beep, beep, beep.

The horn on the bus goes
beep, beep, beep,
all through the town!

The wipers on the bus go
swish, swish, swish,
swish, swish, swish,
swish, swish, swish.

The wipers on the bus go
swish, swish, swish,
all through the town!

The motor on the bus goes
zoom, zoom, zoom,
zoom, zoom, zoom,
zoom, zoom, zoom.

The motor on the bus goes
zoom, zoom, zoom,
all through the town!

The babies on the bus go
waa, waa, waa,
waa, waa, waa,
waa, waa, waa.

The babies on the bus go
waa, waa, waa,
all through the town!

The parents on the bus go
shush, shush, shush,
shush, shush, shush,
shush, shush, shush.

The parents on the bus go
shush, shush, shush,
all through the town!

The wheels on the bus go
round and round,
round and round,
round and round.

The wheels on the bus go
round and round,
all through the town!

Americana
Steven C Music

Wheels on the Bus

Verse 2
The people on the bus go up and down,
up and down, up and down.
The people on the bus go up and down,
all through the town!

Verse 3
The horn on the bus goes beep, beep, beep,
beep, beep, beep, beep, beep.
The horn on the bus goes beep, beep, beep,
all through the town!

Verse 4
The wipers on the bus go swish, swish, swish,
swish, swish, swish, swish, swish, swish.
The wipers on the bus go swish, swish, swish,
all through the town!

Verse 5
The motor on the bus goes zoom, zoom, zoom,
zoom, zoom, zoom, zoom, zoom, zoom.
The motor on the bus goes zoom, zoom, zoom,
all through the town!

Verse 6
The babies on the bus go waa, waa, waa,
waa, waa, waa, waa, waa, waa.
The babies on the bus go waa, waa, waa,
all through the town!

Verse 7
The parents on the bus go shush, shush, shush,
shush, shush, shush, shush, shush, shush.
The parents on the bus go shush, shush, shush,
all through the town!

Verse 8
The wheels on the bus go round and round,
round and round, round and round.
The wheels on the bus go round and round,
all through the town!

GLOSSARY

motor—the part of a car or bus that makes it go

wiper—a part on the outside of a car or bus that wipes water away so the driver can see

GUIDED READING ACTIVITIES

1. Pretend you are on a bus. Come up with the next thing that happens on the bus.

2. Why do you think the parents on the bus go "shush, shush, shush?"

3. Draw a picture of the bus. Then make a map of where it might be going.

TO LEARN MORE

Cabrera, Jane. *The Wheels on the Bus*. New York: Holiday House, 2012.

Crow, Melissa Melton. *Lucky School Bus*. Mankato, MN: Stone Arch Books, 2012.

Dean, James. *Pete the Cat: The Wheels on the Bus*. New York: HarperCollins, 2013.

Lassieur, Allison. *Buses in Action*. Mankato, MN: Capstone Press, 2011.